DOES A SEAL SMILE?

Fred Ehrlich, M.D.
Pictures by Emily Bolam

Blue Apple Books

Maplewood, N.J.

Text copyright © 2006 by Fred Ehrlich
Illustrations copyright © 2006 by Emily Bolam
All rights reserved
CIP Data is available.
First published in the United States 2006 by
🍎 Blue Apple Books
P.O. Box 1380, Maplewood, N.J. 07040
www.blueapplebooks.com

Distributed in the U.S. by Chronicle Books
Printed in China

ISBN 13: 978-1-59354-169-9
ISBN 10: 1-59354-169-4

1 3 5 7 9 10 8 6 4 2

Does a seal smile?

No.
A seal doesn't smile.

A seal can bark and
flap its flippers when
it sees another seal.

Does a mandrill smile?

Not exactly.
This mandrill's expression is really more
snarl than smile. He is opening his mouth
and showing his teeth to show he is angry.

Does a coyote smile?

Not really.

Coyotes use facial
expressions to communicate,
but they do not smile.

Does a chimp smile?

Almost.

Chimpanzees are very social animals with many different facial expressions and sounds.

Chimps greet other chimps in many different ways;
a person who gets to know chimps learns what
the chimp means by the position of the chimp's tail,
arms, legs—its whole body.

This chimp's body says:
"I'm glad to see you!"

This one's body says:
"Go away. Don't bother me!"

But no animal has as many ways of greeting another member of its species as a human being.

When a baby is six weeks old, it smiles when it sees another person.

At six months, the baby smiles and waves its arms and kicks its legs when it sees a familiar face. The baby shows he is excited and happy.

At around nine months,
the baby sometimes shows that
she doesn't know you with
an unfriendly expression.

A year-old baby can
wave bye-bye.

And soon after the baby
will speak and say,
"Hi!"

Small children give hugs and
kisses when they greet
people they know.

And when they *see* people they don't know,
they sometimes hide their faces.

People use many more ways to greet
each other than animals.
They use lots of different expressions:

They can shake hands.

Slap a high five.

Hug each other.

People greet each other differently in different countries.

In Korea they bow slightly and shake hands.

In Japan they bow to each other.

In France they kiss once on each cheek.

In Greece they wave "hello."

In some places men and women greet each other differently.

Pakistan

Egypt

India

Saudi Arabia

How do you greet someone you know?